This book belongs to

....

Let's learn some vocabulary included in the story

Amir: It's the name of the little boy, it means prince in Arabic.

Prophet Yusuf: is a prophet mentioned in the Quran.

(S.W.T): stands for the Arabic words "Subhanahu wa ta'ala." Muslims use these or similar words to glorify God when mentioning his name.

Al Khaliq: means The Creator, one of the Names of Allah.

Bismillah: is a phrase in Arabic meaning "in the name of God".

Alhamdulillah: is an Arabic phrase meaning "praise be to God".

Dua: means invocation, it is an act of supplication.

بِسْمِ اللهِ الرَّحْمٰنِ الرَّحِيمِ

Amir waited for his mommy to come. It was his favorite time of the day. He loved listening to his mommy's bedtime stories before going to bed. His mommy would tell him a different story every day.

She told him stories of the great prophets; their trials and tribulations. She would also tell him stories of the greatness of Allah (S.W.T).

But a question always lingered in Amir's mind now and then. He was hesitant to talk about it in front of his parents. He didn't know what response he would get from them. But today, he decided to clear everything in his mind.

Mommy entered his room and smiled at Amir.

"Amir, my son. I see you are excited about today's story," said Mommy with a kind

smile. Amir nodded excitedly and Mommy kissed the top of his head.

"Today I will tell you about a dream, Amir," said Mommy as she tucked little Amir

in his bed.

Amir frowned.

"Whose dream, Mommy?" he inquired, curious.

"I will tell you about a dream Prophet Yusuf had," replied Mommy.

"But Mommy," said Amir as he frowned.

"Is something bothering you, my son?" Mommy asked.

"Mommy. Who is Allah?" replied Amir after a while. "We start every action after saying "in the name of Allah, Bismillah" We thank Him after we eat food and we go to sleep thinking of Him. We wake up thanking Him for keeping us alive, we always say Alhamdulillah. But you never told who is HE?"

Mommy looked at him for a while. She then smiled and took Amir's hands and kissed them.

"My son! The apple of my eyes. Who made you and me? Allah (S.W.T)! Who created the stars, the sky, the ground, and everything around us? Allah!

Everything happens after His order.

He is the Creator and The Sustainer,

Allah is Al Khaliq" Mommy replied lovingly.

"Thanks to Allah, there are a lot of animals in nature"

"Planets, the Sun and many stars"

"Oceans, seas with lots of fish and other wonderful creatures" Mommy added.

Amir looked confused.

"Wait a minute, Amir," Mommy said as she went out of the room.

She came back with a piece of cotton on a plate. She put some drops of water on the cotton and placed a bean in it.

"Now wait for a few days and then see," Mommy said as she smiled. She placed the plate on the big table.

"Let us thank Our God, Allah for this day." Said Mommy as she continued to say the Dua before going to sleep.

Amir woke up every day to look at the piece of cotton to see a change, but he didn't see anything. One day, he saw little green sprouts arising from the bean.

"Mommy! Mommy!" Amir called out to his mother in excitement.

Mommy came into the room and after seeing the sprouts, smiled.

"You see. Little Amir. Allah (S.W.T) ordered these sprouts to grow from this bean. It wouldn't have grown without Allah's permission. He has control over everything in this world. He is responsible for the life of someone even as tiny as a newborn ant.

You saw your pictures as an infant. Only Allah's permission allowed you to grow into a lovely and handsome boy," Mommy said, as she stroked Amir's cheeks lovingly.

Amir's eyes widened with admiration.

"It means we should thank Allah every second of our lives," he said, looking at his mommy for approval.

Mommy laughed.

"Yes, and we should obey his commands and orders too. So, He considers us one of His beloved slaves," Mommy added.

Amir smiled and vowed to become a good Muslim.

We hope your children enjoyed this little story. Please leave us a comment on the Amazon website. Your opinion is very important to us. May Allah bless you.

Printed in the USA
CPSIA information can be obtained
at www.ICGtesting.com
LVHW072147051224
798473LV00029B/187